TO MOM, DAD AND KATHRYN:

Not a day goes by that I don't think of you.

www.mascotbooks.com

WHEN YOU SEE A BLUEBIRD

For more information, please contact:
Mascot Books
620 Herndon Parkway, Suite 320
Herndon, VA 20170
info@mascotbooks.com

Library of Congress Control Number: 2020909208

CPSIA Code: PRTWP0720A
ISBN-13: 978-1-64543-504-4

Printed in South Korea

When You See
a Bluebird

MARY VEROXIE HEATER

Illustrated by
Rana Wijaya Soemadi

When you see a
BLUEBIRD, that's
me saying hi

When you see a
BUTTERFLY,
that's me flying by

When you see a beautiful FLOWER,
that's me watching you play

When you see a
BEE, that's me
listening to what
you say

When you see a DEER,
that's me making you smile

When you see an ANT,
that's me marching with style

When you see a
RAINBOW, that's
me brightening up
your day

When you see a
FIREFLY, that's
just me lighting up
the way

When you play in the
LEAVES, that's me
floating by

When you build a
SNOWMAN, that's
me being sly

When you put on a
GLOVE, that's me
holding your hand

When you walk on the **BEACH**, those are my footprints in the sand

When you hear the wind **BLOW**,
that's me calling your name

When you hear the rain **FALL**, that's me playing a game

When you hear THUNDER, that's me being sad

When you hear the OCEAN,
that's me making you glad

When you hear my favorite SONG, that's me making you wiggle

When you watch my favorite MOVIE,
that's me making you giggle.

When you smell
cookies BAKING,
that's me with a
treat

When you smell
my favorite
FLOWER,
that's me being
sweet

When you feel a cozy
BLANKET, that's me
keeping you warm

When you feel **SAFE AND SOUND,** that's me protecting you from harm

I know I had to say **GOODBYE**, but please don't you cry

Because when you see a
BLUEBIRD, know that's me,
always by your side

ABOUT THE AUTHOR

Mary Veroxie Heater is a special education teacher in Montgomery County, Maryland. This is her first children's book, inspired by her love of reading and her own childhood experiences. She lost her parents and younger sister, Kathryn, well before their time. Born and raised on Long Island, New York, she lives in Maryland with her husband Robert and their son Leo, who loves books.

ABOUT THE ILLUSTRATOR

Art has been a part of Rana's life since childhood. Born in Semarang, Central Java, Indonesia, she loves making and illustrating stories. She has already made an independent novel and two comics. She hopes that one day her dreams will come true: owning her own house and art studio, and of course, lots of children's books written and illustrated by her!

[O] @ranadigipaint

✉ rana.digitalpainting@gmail.com